Dear Parents:

Congratulations! Your child is taking the first steps on an exciting journey. The destination? Independent reading!

STEP INTO READING® will help your child get there. The program offers five steps to reading success. Each step includes fun stories and colorful art or photographs. In addition to original fiction and books with favorite characters, there are Step into Reading Non-Fiction Readers, Phonics Readers and Boxed Sets, Sticker Readers, and Comic Readers—a complete literacy program with something to interest every child.

Learning to Read, Step by Step!

Ready to Read Preschool–Kindergarten
• big type and easy words • rhyme and rhythm • picture clues
For children who know the alphabet and are eager to begin reading.

Reading with Help Preschool–Grade 1
• basic vocabulary • short sentences • simple stories
For children who recognize familiar words and sound out new words with help.

Reading on Your Own Grades 1–3
• engaging characters • easy-to-follow plots • popular topics
For children who are ready to read on their own.

Reading Paragraphs Grades 2–3
• challenging vocabulary • short paragraphs • exciting stories
For newly independent readers who read simple sentences with confidence.

Ready for Chapters Grades 2–4
• chapters • longer paragraphs • full-color art
For children who want to take the plunge into chapter books but still like colorful pictures.

STEP INTO READING® is designed to give every child a successful reading experience. The grade levels are only guides; children will progress through the steps at their own speed, developing confidence in their reading.

Remember, a lifetime love of reading starts with a single step!

Step into Reading, Random House, and the Random House colophon are registered trademarks of Penguin Random House LLC.

Visit us on the Web!
StepIntoReading.com
rhcbooks.com

Educators and librarians, for a variety of teaching tools, visit us at RHTeachersLibrarians.com

ISBN 978-0-7364-4358-6 (trade) — ISBN 978-0-7364-9032-0 (lib. bdg.)
ISBN 978-0-7364-4359-3 (ebook)

Printed in the United States of America

10 9 8 7 6 5 4 3 2 1

Tiana's Garden Grows

by Bria Alston

illustrated by the Disney Storybook Art Team

Random House New York

Tiana wants to make
a new meal.

It is call jambalaya!

She needs ghost peppers.

But ghost peppers are
from India.
Tiana writes a letter
to a farm in India.

She asks for some
seeds for the peppers.

A few weeks later, Naveen
brings Tiana a letter.
The seeds from the
farm arrived!

It is time to learn
how to grow them.
She will need a garden.

Tiana goes to the market.
She buys special gloves
for gardening.

She cleans the roof
of Tiana's Palace.
It is a perfect place
for the garden!

Tiana pours dirt
into a pot.
Next, she puts
in the seeds.

Then she waters
the dirt.
Now she must wait.

The peppers will grow soon.
Tiana is excited
to see them!
She plants
other seeds.

Naveen wants to
grow something, too!

He asks Tiana how
seeds become vegetables.

Tiana shows him.
She cuts open
a cucumber and
pulls out the seeds.
She cleans the seeds.
They are ready to plant!

Now Louis wants to grow vegetables!

He plants radishes.
They grow and grow
and grow!

Charlotte wants
to grow flowers.
She does not want
to get dirty.

Tiana shows her
what to do.
They plant pretty
flowers together.

There are pots all over
the rooftop.

The garden has
many vegetables!

That night, Tiana makes
everyone jambalaya.
It is the perfect
summer dinner!